Black *Spot*

Sandra Woodcock

Published in association with
The Basic Skills Agency

Hodder & Stoughton
A MEMBER OF THE HODDER HEADLINE GROUP

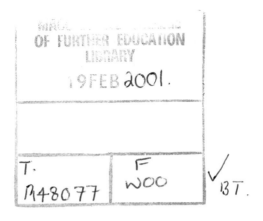
Order queries: please contact Bookpoint Ltd, 39 Milton Park, Abingdon, Oxon
OX14 4TD. Telephone: (44) 01235 400414, Fax: (44) 1235 400454.
Lines are open from 9.00-6.00, Monday to Saturday, with a 24 hour message answering
service. Email address: orders@bookpoint.co.uk

British Library Cataloguing in Publication Data

Woodcock, Sandra
   Black spot. – (Chillers) (Livewire)
   1. Readers – English fiction
   I. Title   II. Basic Skills Agency
   428.6

ISBN 0 340 697539

First published 1997
Impression number   10 9 8 7 6 5 4
Year   2002 2001 2000 1999

Typeset by Fakenham Photosetting Ltd, Fakenham, Norfolk.
Printed in Great Britain for Hodder & Stoughton Educational,
a division of Hodder Headline Plc, 338 Euston Road, London NW1 3BH
by Athenæum Press Ltd, Gateshead, Tyne & Wear.

Black Spot

Contents

1

Crashes in April

Tim Foster died in a car crash.

It was on a sunny April morning.

His car left the road and turned over.

It burst into flames.

No-one knew why it happened.

There were no other cars.

The road was dry.

The car was almost new.

Tim was a careful driver.

So why had the car crashed?

A week later there was a second accident.

It was in the same place.

A car braked very hard.

A motorbike ran into the back of it.

The car driver was in shock.

He could remember nothing.

So no-one knew why he had braked.

A policeman had a good look

at where the crash happened.

He didn't find anything.

PC Alan Wood was writing a report.

It was about the two accidents.

He put the dates into a computer.

He looked back at last year's accidents.

All the dates were on the screen.

There were three car crashes last year.

They were all in the same week.

All at the same spot.

All at the same time – early in the morning.

PC Wood checked the computer.

Were there any other car crashes there

last year?

No.

Not even in bad weather.

Not even at busy times.

He looked back to other years.

The road was new. It was a bypass.

It had opened five years ago.

PC Wood looked at the computer.

Each year at the same spot

there had been a car crash.

They all took place in early April.

2

PC Wood Asks Questions

PC Wood talked to other policemen.

'It's just one of those things,' said PC Smith.

'It happens like that. Accident black spots.

You can look and look

but you won't find anything.'

'Yes,' said PC Wood. 'But these happen
in the same week each year.'

'It could just be chance,'
said PC Smith.

'I think I'll check some more,'
said PC Wood.

'I find it spooky.'

He checked the computer.

How many car crashes had been fatal?

Most of them had been.

But two years ago a car had crashed
into a minibus.

The minibus driver had not died.

PC Wood found his name.

He was John Day.

He lived at 52 Red Street.

'Right,' said PC Wood to himself.

He went to see John Day.

He told him why he had come.

'What can you tell me about the crash?'

he asked.

John Day said,

'I was driving along. It was quiet.

The road was empty. Then I saw a blue car.

It was coming towards me.

A woman was driving.

Suddenly she swerved.

She left her side of the road.

She was coming right at me.

I couldn't do anything.

Her car smashed into me.

I think I passed out.

Then I heard people shouting.

A man pulled me out of the minibus.

There were police cars and an ambulance.

Then I passed out again.

'Why did the woman swerve?' asked PC Wood.

John Day shook his head.

'I'm not sure. But I can still see her face.

She looked shocked.

As if she had seen something

in the road.'

'Was there something in the road?'

PC Wood asked.

'No, nothing.' said John Day.

'The road was clear.

I'm sure of that.'

'Thank you,' said PC Wood.

PC Wood went back to the station.

He went to the computer.

In the last crash a boy on a motorbike

had been killed. But the car driver

was alive. His name was Mark West.

3

Old Harry

PC Wood went to see him.

He was still in hospital.

The doctor said, 'Don't stay too long.'

PC Wood spoke gently.

Mark West was only a young man.

He was still in shock.

'Why did you brake so hard?' he asked.

'One moment the road was empty.

Then I saw this old man.

He was in the middle of the road.

I don't know where he came from.

I was going to hit him.'

'Tell me what he was like,' said PC Wood.

'He had a spade and rake,' said Mark.

'He looked like a gardener.

He wore brown cord trousers.

He had a jacket, shirt and tie on.

And a blue hat.

He must have been a gardener.

He looked just like a gardener!'

'In the middle of the road?' asked PC Wood.

Mark was upset. It was time to go.

'Try to rest,' said PC Wood. 'Don't worry.'

That night PC Wood went out for a drink.

He went to a village pub.

He had not been to the pub before.

It was near the accident spot.

He talked to lots of people.

He asked about the old man.

The old man with the jacket and tie.

The gardener.

At last someone said,

'You mean, old Harry.

He's dead now.

Go and see Jessie at Rose Cottage.

She'll tell you about him.'

17

4

Jessie

The next day PC Wood went to Rose Cottage.

Jessie was an old lady.

She lived by herself.

'Yes. I can tell you about Harry,' she said.

'He was my brother. He lived here with me.'

'What happened to him?' asked PC Wood.

'He died five years ago,' she said.

PC Wood looked out of the window.

The road was close to the house.

It was where the accidents happened.

'Don't be upset by this,' he said.

'Someone says he saw Harry.

It was the other day. Down there.'

PC Wood pointed to the road.

Jessie wasn't upset.

'Oh yes,' she said.

'I see him down there too.

At this time of year.'

'But how? Why?' said PC Wood.

'Well,' said Jessie. 'It was his garden.

Before they made the road.'

'Harry loved his garden.

All his life he loved that garden.

But they made him sell it.

They wanted the land for the road.

He was so upset. He never got over it.

I bet that's what killed him.

It broke his heart.

I'm not surprised to see him.

In April he always started his digging.

He started his seed beds.

Look there he is now!'

PC Wood looked out of the window.

He went cold all over.

In the middle of the road was an old man.

An old man wearing a blue hat.

He was starting to dig.

PC Wood closed his eyes.

He couldn't see what was happening.

But he could hear the scream of car horns.